The GINGERBREAD MAN

LOOSE at the ZOO

Laura Murray

Illustrated by Mike Lowery

G. P. PUTNAM'S SONS

To Lisa and Mark—my TGBS and TGBB!
I'm so grateful for your support, advice,
and encouragement through the years.
I'm lucky to be your TGLS!
-L.M.

For Allister and Katrin,
who make life pretty awesome.
—M.L.

G. P. PUTNAM'S SONS
an imprint of Penguin Random House LLC
375 Hudson Street, New York, NY 10014

Text copyright © 2016 by Laura Murray.
Illustrations copyright © 2016 by Mike Lowery.
Penguin supports copyright. Copyright fuels creativity, encourages diverse voices,
promotes free speech, and creates a vibrant culture. Thank you for buying
an authorized edition of this book and for complying with copyright laws by not reproducing,
scanning, or distributing any part of it in any form without permission. You are supporting
writers and allowing Penguin to continue to publish books for every reader.

G. P. Putnam's Sons is a registered trademark of Penguin Random House LLC.

Library of Congress Cataloging-in-Publication Data
Murray, Laura, 1970-
The gingerbread man loose at the zoo / Laura Murray ; illustrated by Mike Lowery.
pages cm
Summary: When the gingerbread man gets separated from his class during a field trip to the zoo,
he uses his teacher's animal scavenger hunt clues to find his way back to them.
[1. Stories in rhyme. 2. Cookies—Fiction. 3. Treasure hunt (Game)—Fiction. 4. Zoos—Fiction.
5. School field trips—Fiction.] I. Lowery, Mike, 1980- illustrator. II. Title.
PZ8.3.M9368Gh 2016 [E]—dc23 2015009122

Manufactured in China by RR Donnelley Asia Printing Solutions Ltd.
ISBN 978-0-399-16867-3
3 5 7 9 10 8 6 4 2

Design by Ryan Thomann.
Text set in Bokka and Dr. Eric, with a bit of hand-lettering.
The illustrations were rendered with pencil, traditional screen printing, and digital color.

I woke to the sound of a rumbling
ROAR!
and hooting,
and howling,
and growling
galore.

I ran to my window to see this strange creature.

GRRR!

Imagine my **shock** when I saw my own
TEACHER!

My **classmates** all giggled.
I joined in
their game.

HEE HEE   HA HA

"HAVE A WILD DAY!" said a man at the front
as we pulled out our riddles to start on the hunt.

RIDDLE # 1

I'm spotted. I'm gentle.
I'm tall as a tree.
A branch full of leaves is
the best snack for me.
I have a new baby,
and she is my calf.

AH-HA!

we all shouted.

"THE ANSWER'S ...

We followed the signs as we raced down the trail,

till we spied her **long legs** and her **thin spotted tail.**

She **scooped** me up high as her tongue curled **around**, but nobody noticed below on the **ground**.

My **classmates** were busily reading clue **two**.

OH, NO, I cried out. SHE'S BEGINNING TO **CHEW!**

I tickled her nose and she let out a sneeze.

ACHOO!

Then I **zoomed** through the air to some **tropical trees.**

A long, loopy **vine** twisted **down** and **around.**
So I whipped up my courage and **swung** to the **ground.**

WEEEE!

I glanced at my paper, then knew what to do—

BY **SOLVING** THE **RIDDLES,** I'LL FIND MY CLASS, **TOO!**

RIDDLE #②

I scurry, I screech,
and I swing from my tail.
I'm hanging around on the
small primate trail.

I love sweet bananas.
I'm feisty and spunky.

I heard a loud **rustle** and turned in **surprise** to a small cheeky **monkey** with curious **eyes**.

He picked at my **buttons**, then tried for my **hat**.

NO WAY, SILLY RASCAL! I CAN'T GIVE YOU **THAT.**

He stayed on my **tail** as I dodged through the **grass**,
but I **squeezed** underneath the tall habitat **glass**.

I waved to the
ZEBRA,

THE RHINO,

The crocodile opened his big

TOOTHY TRAP.

He eyed me like
I'd make a good ginger **SNAP!**

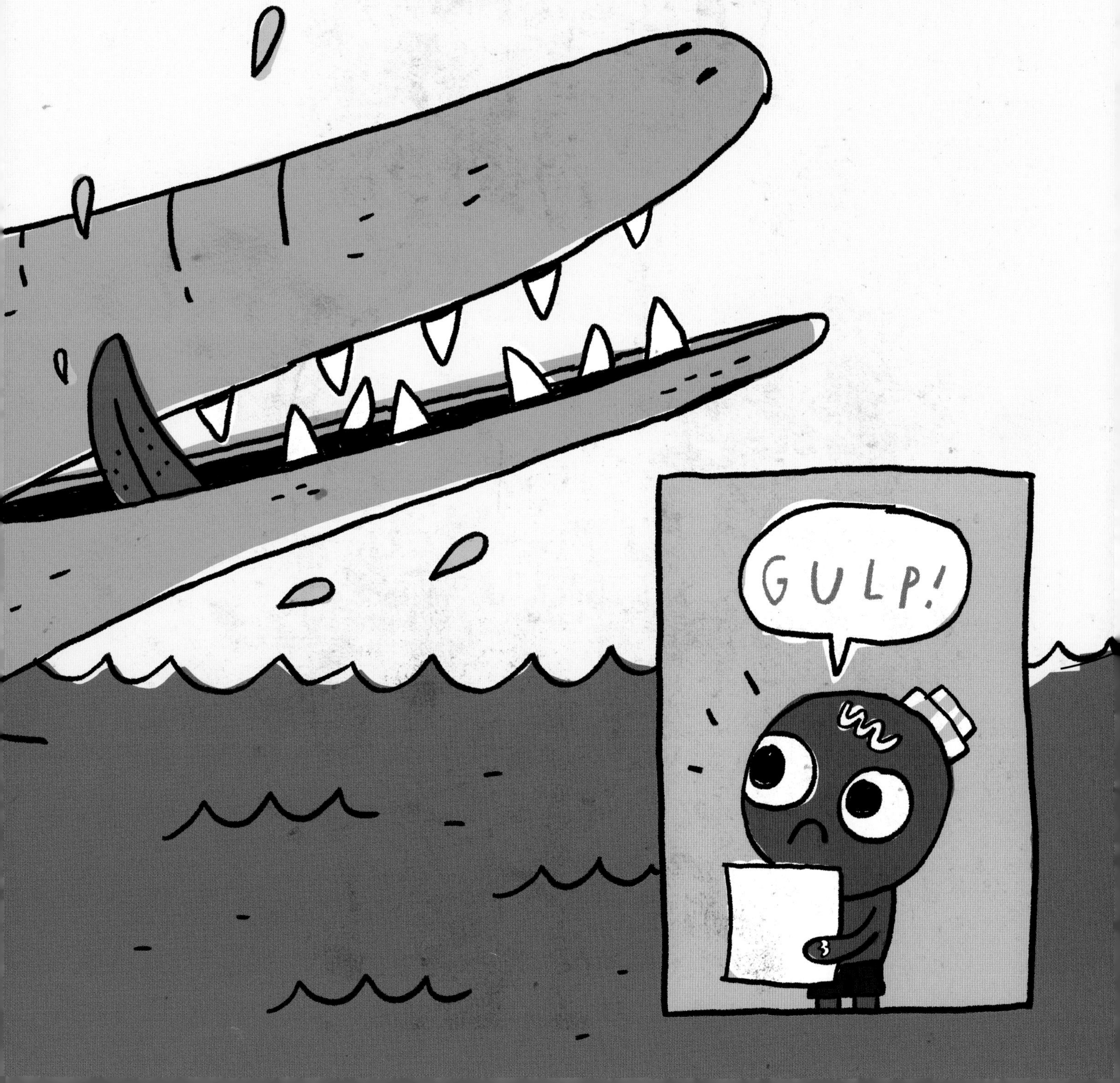

I **raced** down the path and my feet fairly **flew.**

Then **out** from a shrub popped a small **kangaroo.**

She started to **whimper,** hopped **this way** and **that,** then **snuffled,** and **shuffled,** and **slumped** as she **sat.**

She opened her **POCKET** and pointed **inside.** I **tucked** myself in and said,

THANKS FOR THE **RIDE!**

WE'LL FOLLOW THE ARROWS THAT SAY KANGAROO. THEY'LL LEAD TO MY CLASSMATES AND YOUR MAMA, TOO!

TOGETHER WE'LL FIND THEM. I KNOW THAT WE CAN! A SMALL KANGAROO AND A *GINGERBREAD MAN!*

We **hopped** down the path to the grassy **savanna** and **spied** a large crowd near the outback **cabana**.

I **popped** from her pocket and jumped to the **ground**.

She sprang to her mom
with a long leaping
bound.

My classmates all pointed and let out a cheer.

WE FOLLOWED THE RIDDLES AND FOUND YOU ALL HERE!

YOU'RE SUCH A SMART COOKIE! YOU HELPED SAVE THE DAY. OUR JOEY GOT LOST, AND YOU SHOWED HER THE WAY.

I'M SO VERY PROUD OF MY SUPER ZOO CREW! NOW IT'S TIME TO HEAD BACK TO OUR HABITAT, TOO.

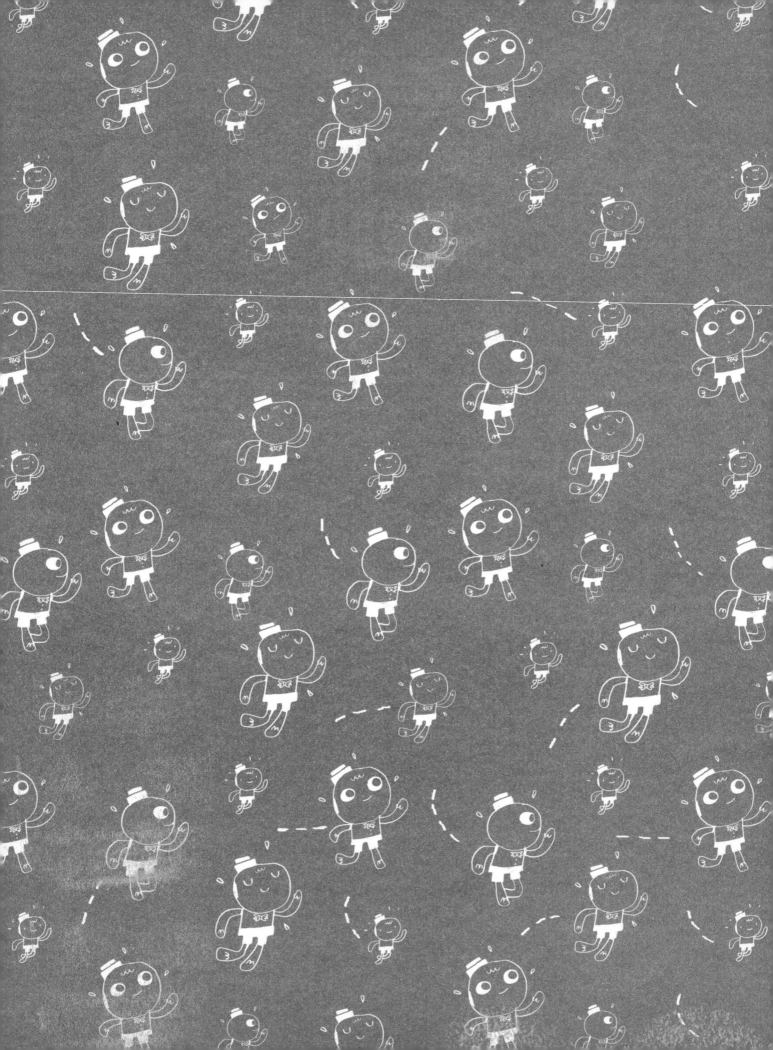